FOND DU LAC PUBLIC LIBRARY

WITHDRAWN

DOGS TO THE RESCUE!
WATER RESCUE DOGS

By Sara Green

BELLWETHER MEDIA • MINNEAPOLIS, MN

Jump into the cockpit and take flight with Pilot books. Your journey will take you on high-energy adventures as you learn about all that is wild, weird, fascinating, and fun!

This edition first published in 2014 by Bellwether Media, Inc.

No part of this publication may be reproduced in whole or in part without written permission of the publisher. For information regarding permission, write to Bellwether Media, Inc., Attention: Permissions Department, 5357 Penn Avenue South, Minneapolis, MN 55419.

Library of Congress Cataloging-in-Publication Data

Green, Sara, 1964-
 Water rescue dogs / by Sara Green.
   pages cm. – (Pilot: Dogs to the rescue!)
 Includes bibliographical references and index.
  Summary: "Engaging images accompany information about water rescue dogs. The combination of high-interest subject matter and narrative text is intended for students in grades 3 through 7"– Provided by publisher.
 ISBN 978-1-60014-961-0 (hardcover : alk. paper)
 1. Water rescue dogs–Juvenile literature. I. Title.
 SF428.55.G74 2014
 636.7'0886–dc23
                                           2013013211

Text copyright © 2014 by Bellwether Media, Inc. PILOT and associated logos are trademarks and/or registered trademarks of Bellwether Media, Inc. SCHOLASTIC, CHILDREN'S PRESS, and associated logos are trademarks and/or registered trademarks of Scholastic Inc.

Printed in the United States of America, North Mankato, MN.

TABLE OF CONTENTS

A Newfoundland to the Rescue!....... 4
What Is a Water Rescue Dog? 6
A Gentle Giant 8
Training for Water Rescue 10
Air Scenting 18
Bilbo: The Lifeguard Dog.............. 20
Glossary 22
To Learn More............................. 23
Index 24

A NEWFOUNDLAND TO THE RESCUE!

A Newfoundland dog named Boo walked with his owner along a California river. The river's **current** was strong. Suddenly, Boo saw a man struggling to stay afloat in the water. The brave dog jumped into the river and swam to the man. Boo grabbed the man's arm and pulled him safely to shore.

The man was very lucky that Boo happened to walk by that day. The man was deaf and did not speak. When he fell into the river, he could not call for help. Boo did not have any training in water rescue. He used his **instincts** to save the man. In 1996, the Newfoundland Club of America awarded Boo a medal for his heroism.

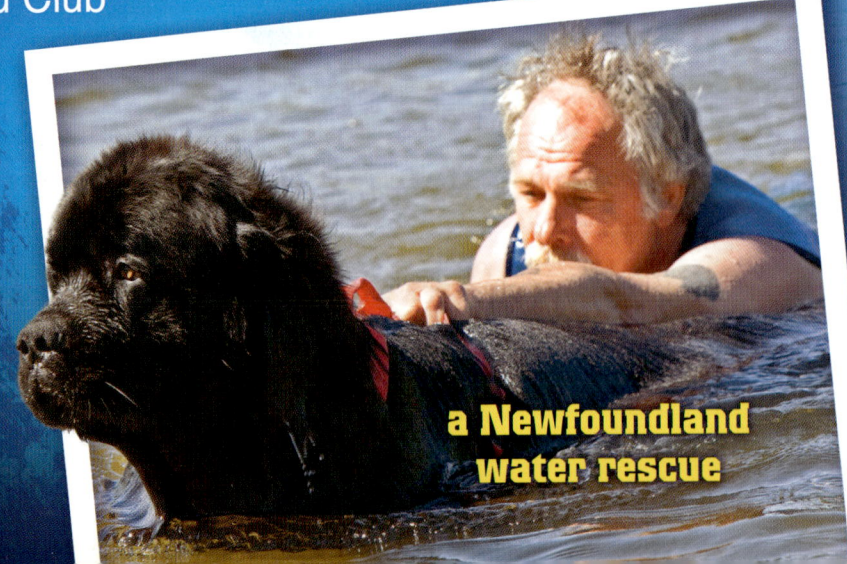

a Newfoundland water rescue

A Ton of Strength! Newfoundlands can pull more than 2,000 pounds (907 kilograms).

WHAT IS A WATER RESCUE DOG?

Water rescue dogs can be seen jumping from boats and running along shorelines. They are specially trained dogs that save people from drowning and other water emergencies. These canine lifeguards often have the ability to do what human lifeguards cannot. Many have the strength to **tow** people and small boats to shore through rough waters.

Many dog breeds can be trained to be water rescue dogs, but large breeds are the best fit for the job. They have the size and strength to do the towing. No matter the breed, all water rescue dogs must be friendly to people and other dogs. **Endurance** is also important. The strongest dogs can swim more than 2 miles (3.2 kilometers) in choppy waters. Above all, water rescue dogs must have plenty of energy and enthusiasm for water activities.

A GENTLE GIANT

The Newfoundland is the most common water rescue breed. This giant dog is gentle, friendly, and has an instinct to rescue people. A Newfoundland has strong muscles and large, **webbed** paws. These help the dog move through the water with ease. It uses its long tail as a **rudder** to change directions in the water.

The Newfoundland's thick waterproof coat protects its skin from cold waters. Its large lungs hold a lot of air. This helps the Newfoundland to swim long distances without losing its breath. The Newfoundland also swims with a breaststroke instead of a dog paddle. This gives it more power in the water.

Other Canine Lifeguards

The Portuguese Water Dog, Leonberger, Labrador Retriever, and Golden Retriever are other common water resuce breeds. These strong, friendly dogs love jumping into the water!

Newfoundland

Breeds of Water Rescue Dogs

 Portuguese Water Dog

 Leonberger

 Labrador Retriever

 Golden Retriever

Profile: Newfoundland

Waterproof Coat
The Newfoundland has a double coat of fur that is water resistant.

Long Tail
The Newfoundland's tail is broad at the base and straight. It acts like a rudder.

Size
Height: 25 to 29 inches (63 to 74 centimeters)

Weight: 100 to 150 pounds (45 to 68 kilograms)

Paws
The Newfoundland has webbed toes for powerful swimming.

TRAINING FOR WATER RESCUE

Water rescue dogs need about three years of training. The dogs train with people called **handlers**. They are usually the dogs' owners as well as water rescue experts. Many water rescue dogs start their training as puppies. First, the puppies learn basic **obedience skills**. They learn how to behave around people and other dogs.

The handlers give the puppies plenty of time in the water. At first, puppies practice retrieving objects from both shallow and deep waters. Next, the handlers encourage the puppies to play with water rescue equipment. This includes boat cushions, floating lines, and life jackets. Puppies also get used to wearing their own life jackets. These will help them stay afloat in deep, rough water later on. The puppies are rewarded with a lot of praise after they enter the water. They also receive toys, treats, or playtime. The pups learn that playing in water with rescue equipment is fun!

A Platform for Paws

Many search boats have a front platform for dogs. The handlers often put floor mats on the platform. They keep a dog's paws cool and prevent them from slipping.

After mastering basic skills, the dogs are ready to learn rescue skills and get **certified** for work. The dogs practice diving from boats and docks. They learn to swim to targets in the water. The dogs retrieve oars and other items and bring them to people in boats.

Water rescue dogs also learn to retrieve small boats. If a boat is drifting, the dogs tow it to shore by pulling on a line. These powerful dogs can tow empty boats or boats with people inside.

A water rescue dog's most important job is to rescue drowning people. Each dog wears a **flotation harness** and has a rescue float attached to its body. To rescue a drowning person, a water rescue dog swims in circles around the person. The dog waits for the person to grab hold of the harness or float, and then it tows the person to land.

rescue float

flotation harness

Water rescue dogs also need to learn what to do when there are multiple **victims**. Sometimes, a dog must decide if one victim is in greater **distress** than the others. If so, the dog quickly brings that person a life preserver first. Many dogs can pull more than one person at a time on a float. The people hang on tightly while they are towed to shore.

Some water rescue dogs face even greater challenges. Dogs with advanced training can rescue an **unconscious** victim. A dog learns to gently grab one of the person's arms with its mouth. The dog then rolls the person face up. This is so the victim can breathe while being towed back to land. These dogs can even rescue an unconscious victim from under a **capsized** boat. A few of the most skilled dogs learn how to leap out of a helicopter into the water. This allows them to quickly aid victims who are far from shore.

A Top Training School

Some of the top water rescue dogs go to school in Italy. The Italian School of Rescue Dogs was the first to train dogs to work from helicopters.

AIR SCENTING

Locating Victims

Air scenting dogs do not need a sample of a person's smell to find them underwater. Instead, they sniff for any human scent and find the point where it is the strongest.

Sometimes water rescue dogs use their outstanding sense of smell to find people who are underwater. Sadly, most of these people are no longer alive. The dogs use a skill called air scenting. People always give off a scent, even when they are underwater. Their scent rises to the surface of the water and then mixes with the air.

When the dogs detect a person's scent in the air, they alert their handlers. They may bark, twirl in place, or paw at the water. Many dogs scratch at the bottom of the boat. No matter how the dogs alert, the handlers know a person may be under the water. Then it is time for a rescue diver to jump in and search!

BILBO: THE LIFEGUARD DOG

A Newfoundland named Bilbo is one of the world's only beach rescue dogs. His owner, Steve Jamieson, worked as a lifeguard on Sennen Beach in England. When Bilbo was a puppy, Steve started training him to perform rescues in the rough English waters. When he was 3 years old, Bilbo started as a lifeguard on Sennen Beach. Over time, Bilbo helped rescue three swimmers from the sea and also helped prevent many beach accidents.

In 2008, the local city council banned all dogs from the beach, including Bilbo. People missed seeing Bilbo on the beach. Many complained to the city council. In time, the city council relaxed the rule. Today, Bilbo spends two days a week on the beach promoting beach safety. Bilbo and Steve also teach beach safety in local schools. In 2010, Bilbo was named Pet Hero of the Year in London. Many people visit Sennen Beach just to see this famous dog!

GLOSSARY

capsized—flipped upside down

certified—proved to have mastery of specific job skills

current—the flow of a body of water

distress—danger or desperate need

endurance—the ability to do something for a long time without stopping

flotation harness—a padded coat that helps a dog float in water; it has handles that a person can grip.

handlers—people who are responsible for highly trained dogs

instincts—natural behaviors of an animal; instincts are not learned.

obedience skills—skills that include sit, stay, come, and down

rudder—a flat, movable object used for steering

tow—to pull behind

unconscious—unaware and unresponsive

victims—people in need of help

webbed—having thin skin connecting the toes

TO LEARN MORE

AT THE LIBRARY
Hengel, Katherine. *Proud Portuguese Water Dogs.* Edina, Minn.: ABDO Pub. Co., 2011.

Ruffin, Frances E. *Water Rescue Dogs.* New York, N.Y.: Bearport Pub. Co., 2006.

Wilcox, Charlotte. *Newfoundlands.* Mankato, Minn.: Capstone Press, 2012.

ON THE WEB
Learning more about water rescue dogs is as easy as 1, 2, 3.

1. Go to www.factsurfer.com.

2. Enter "water rescue dogs" into the search box.

3. Click the "Surf" button and you will see a list of related Web sites.

With factsurfer.com, finding more information is just a click away.

INDEX

air scenting, 18, 19
alerts, 19
awards, 4, 20
Bilbo, 20
Boo, 4
breeds, 4, 7, 8, 9, 20
certification, 12
characteristics, 7, 8, 9
duties, 7, 14, 15
equipment, 10, 12, 14, 15
handlers, 10, 12, 19
history, 4, 20
instincts, 4, 8
Italian School of Rescue Dogs, 17
Jamieson, Steve, 20
Newfoundland Club of America, 4
Newfoundlands, 4, 5, 8, 9, 20

rewards, 10
safety, 20
Sennen Beach, 20
sense of smell, 19
skills, 10, 12, 13, 16, 19
strength, 5, 7, 8, 13
training, 10, 12, 13, 15, 16, 17, 20

The images in this book are reproduced through the courtesy of: Eric Isselee, front cover (left), p. 9 (bottom); Greg Flume/ Stringer/ Getty Images, front cover, p. 18; Juniors Bildarchiv/ Glow Images, p. 4; Stockfolio/ Alamy, p. 5; tony french/ Alamy, pp. 6, 17; Marco Clarizia, p. 7; NaturePL/ SuperStock, p. 8; Lee319, p. 9 (left); hopsalka, p. 9 (middle left); Gerald Marella, p. 9 (middle right); Jan S., p. 9 (right); Claudiu Marius Pascalina, p. 11; CB2/ ZOB/ WENN/ Newscom, pp. 12-13, 14, 16; Biosphoto/ SuperStock, p. 13; seraficus, p. 15; Michalrasovsky, p. 19; Ian Wilson, p. 21.